Showdown at
camp
wannaweep

Adapted by Kiki Thorpe

Based on the series created by

Mark McCorkle & Bob Schooley

Watch it on

New York

First Edition
3 5 7 9 10 8 6 4 2

Library of Congress Catalog Card Number: 2002095479

ISBN 0-7868-4587-2
For more Disney Press fun, visit www.disneybooks.com
Visit DisneyChannel.com

CHAPTER 1

Next Stop: Nowhere

Kim Possible sat in the back of a speeding school bus. Outside the window, a pine forest flashed by in a blur of green. Kim barely saw it. She was too busy getting ready for her latest challenge. The Middleton High School pep squad was on its way to a cheerleading competition. Kim and the other cheerleaders were getting in some last-minute practice.

"Go, Mad Dogs! Go, go, Mad Dogs! Go,

3

Mad Dogs! Go, go, Mad Dogs!" they hollered. "Go, Mad Dogs! Go, go, Mad Dogs! Go, Mad Dogs! Go, go, Mad Dogs! Go, Mad Dogs! Go, go, Mad Dogs!"

Behind the wheel, Mr. Barkin, their teacher, gritted his teeth. He'd been listening to the same cheer for three hours! He glared over his shoulder at the gaggle of go-getters in the seats behind him. "Let's save some pep for the competition, ladies," he snapped.

"Go, Mad Dogs! Go, go, Mad Dogs!" the girls shouted in reply.

In the very back row of the bus, Ron Stoppable bobbed his head along with the

beat. Ron was going to
be the school mascot
in the competition.
As the cheerleaders
shouted, he picked
up a mask that looked
like an angry bulldog
and plopped it on his head.

Mr. Barkin saw him in the rearview mirror. "Stoppable . . ." he warned.

But Ron didn't hear him. "Aaarrr-
oooooooo!" he howled. The cheerleaders
stopped cheering and looked at him. Ron
howled again. He foamed at the mouth like a
rabid dog. When he shook his head, spit flew
everywhere. Ron *loved* being a mascot.

The cheerleaders, however, were not so
thrilled. "Kim, he's doing it again!" Bonnie, a
member of the squad, whined.

Kim winced. Ron was her best friend, but
Kim had to admit that his drooling mad-dog

act was totally uncool. She leaned over the back of her seat, trying to get his attention. "Ron," she said gently. Ron just slobbered and howled. "Ron," Kim said louder. *"Ron!"*

Ron pulled off the mask. "What?" he asked.

"You should, uh, hold back . . ." Kim suggested. "Until the competition. You know, pace yourself."

"Can't hold back, K.P.," Ron replied. "The Mad Dog came to play."

"Yeah!" squeaked Rufus, sticking his thumb in the air. Rufus was Ron's pet naked

mole rat. He went everywhere with Ron.

"No!" Kim said, turning Rufus's thumb toward the ground. She leaned closer to Ron so that the other cheerleaders wouldn't

hear. "Ron, you're already on thin ice with these girls," she whispered. "Can you just try to be somewhat normal?"

Ron folded his arms and stuck out his lower lip. "Is there anyone who is not the boss of me?" he asked.

"I'm *so* not bossy," Kim said.

"Except when you're telling me what to do," Ron replied.

Rufus nodded. "Um-hum, bossy," he agreed.

Kim crossed her arms and turned back

around in her seat. "Hey, you've gotta admit, I usually know what's best," she said.

"Oh, please. Are you kidding me?" Ron said. Kim Possible, teen superhero, wouldn't be here today if it weren't for Ron's help. He had saved her from some of the world's most vile villains. At least that was how Ron saw it. He was just about to lecture Kim . . . when suddenly he looked out the window.

"Wait a minute," Ron said. "This road looks familiar. Too familiar!" He reached over the seat and grabbed Kim's Kim-municator. "Wade, I need a GPS lock on

 our position!" he cried.

Wade, the ten-year-old genius who helped Kim and Ron on their world-saving missions, appeared on the Kimmunicator's screen. "Okay, calm down, Mad Dog," Wade said. He began typing into his computer. "Locked," he said, a second later.

A digital map appeared on the screen of the Kimmunicator. It showed the position of the bus on a curving mountain road. Right next to it was a patch of forest labeled CAMP WANNAWEEP.

Ron gasped. "That can't be right. That can't be right!" he cried. Beneath his freckles, his face turned white as a ghost.

"Ron?" Kim said.

"It's— it's—my— my—my— my worst nightmare!" Ron stuttered.

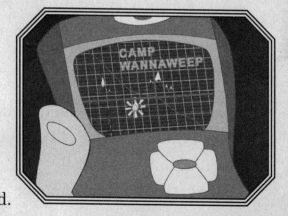

The bulldog mask fell from his hands and rolled down the aisle of the bus. Rufus dove for cover in Ron's pocket. Ron clutched his face and screamed, "Return to Camp Wannaweep!"

Mr. Barkin glanced in the rearview mirror. "Stoppable, do you have a problem?" he barked.

"Drive!" Ron shouted. "Drive fast, Mr. Barkin. Drive like my life depends on it."

Mr. Barkin scowled. "What are you yammering about?" he asked.

"It was the worst summer of all time!"

Ron said. "I swore I'd never come back to Camp Wannaweep. Never!"

Suddenly—*BLAM! BLAM!* The bus's tires blew out! The cheerleaders screamed as the bus swerved across the road.

Mr. Barkin yanked the steering wheel left and right, trying to keep the bus from crashing into the trees. "No bus wipes out on Steve Barkin's watch!" he growled. At last the bus screeched to a halt on the side of the road. Mr. Barkin turned around in his seat to

check his passengers. "Sound off if you're hurtin'," he ordered.

"I'm okay." "Fine." "We're all right," the cheerleaders all said at once.

Ron looked out the window. They had stopped on a dirt road that led into the woods. The bus's headlights lit up a carved wooden sign: CAMP WANNAWEEP.

Ron whimpered. "I'm hurting," he said.

CHAPTER 2

Boss Man Ron

Mr. Barkin crouched on his hands and knees beneath the bus, examining the damage. The right front and rear tires were as flat as fried eggs. "Dandy," Mr. Barkin said grumpily.

"We've got two flat tires," he announced, climbing back onto the bus. "Better call for help."

"Ladies . . . cell phones!" Bonnie commanded.

13

Together, the cheerleaders whipped out their cells and hit the POWER buttons. Nothing happened.

"No service?" they squawked in disbelief.

Bonnie jabbed at the keypad on her phone, but it was no use. The phone was dead. With a snarl of frustration, she sent it flying.

"That's weird," Kim said. She punched the buttons on her Kimmunicator. Usually the Kimmunicator worked everywhere— even Siberia! But now the screen stayed mysteriously blank. "Well, the Kimmunicator isn't working, either," she announced.

"Stoppable," Mr. Barkin said to Ron. "You know the lay of the land?"

Ron shuddered. "Every rock, every tree, every bloodthirsty tick. It haunts me," he said.

"Good. Where's the phone?" Mr. Barkin asked.

Ron's eyes glazed over. He remembered calling home from Camp Wannaweep's only phone. "Mom, hey, it's me again," the eight-year-old Ron had said. "Yeah, yeah, yeah, I know I just called three minutes ago. But I just wanted to ask one more time . . . *Can you, please, get me out of here?!*"

Ron shook his head, trying to erase the awful memory. "I seem to recall a pay phone," he told Mr. Barkin.

"Lead the way," Mr. Barkin said.

Ron cowered in his seat. "Mr. Barkin, I am not—" he began. Suddenly, his eyes opened wide. "What did you say?"

"I said, 'Lead the way,'" Mr. Barkin replied gruffly.

Ron leaped to his feet. "Yeah, this is it," he said. "The one time that Ron Stoppable gets to lead, gets to call the shots, gets to be the big boss man."

Kim rolled her eyes. "Ron, please, just take us to the pay phone," she said.

Ron grinned at her. "Oh, I will," he said. "But you need to understand this: I am your

only hope."

"What? Ron, *normal*," Kim reminded him.

"Listen up, people!" Ron shouted. "Camp Wannaweep is a dangerous and

wicked place. And among us, only I, Ron
Stoppable, know how to survive here."

The cheerleaders stared at Ron. Bonnie
glared at Kim. And Kim hid her face in her
hands. If this was Ron's idea of normal, it
was going to be a very long trip.

Ron waved his arms like a flight attendant,
directing everyone off the bus. "Don't believe
me?" Ron asked when they were all outside.
He pointed to a leafy green plant. "Poison
oak!" he declared smugly. "How do I know?"

Ron recalled the day that he had inno-
cently plucked a leaf of poison oak, asking,

17

"What's this plant?" Hours later, he'd been covered head to toe with the itchiest, most miserable rash known to Ron-kind. Ron's hair stood on end just thinking about it.

"This is a place of evil," he warned the cheerleaders and Mr. Barkin. "Stay close and you'll stay alive." He flicked on his flashlight and started down the road to Camp Wannaweep. Rolling their eyes, Mr. Barkin and the cheerleaders followed him.

But when they reached the pay phone, the receiver was dangling off the hook. Kim tried several times, but she couldn't get a dial tone. The line was dead. "Out of order," she reported.

Mr. Barkin looked around the camp. The cabins were dark and empty. Some of the buildings were missing windows. It looked like no one had been there for years. "I don't like this," he said.

"Place of ev-i-l-l-l-l," Ron said.

Tara, a cheerleader with crinkly blond hair and big blue eyes, clutched Kim's arm. "This is just like those movies," she said. "Innocent teens . . . stranded at a camp in the middle of nowhere . . . then some creepo starts to pick them off. One by one."

Kim shook off Tara's hand. "*So* not the drama, Tara. This isn't a horror movie," she said impatiently.

"Oh, isn't it?" Ron asked. He held his flashlight under his chin. His face lit up like a spooky jack-o'-lantern.

Bonnie wrinkled her nose. "Okay, if this were a horror movie, there would be more guys. And they'd be way cuter than him," she said, pointing at Ron.

"Oh, Bonnie, you remind me of the cruel kids at camp," Ron said sadly, shaking his head. "Sticks and stones."

Tara's blue eyes opened wide. "They called you names?" she asked.

"Yes. While they were hitting me with sticks and stones," Ron said.

Suddenly, a cheerleader named Crystal gasped and pointed at the bushes. "I saw something move!" she cried.

Kim grabbed Ron's flashlight and shone it on the spot. The beam caught a little squirrel red-handed in

the act of grabbing a nut. With a flick of its tail, it darted into the bushes.

"It's just a squirrel," Kim said.

"*Just* a squirrel? Really?" Ron said skeptically. He told the group about the time he'd been cornered by a pack of Camp Wannaweep's  snarling, razor-toothed squirrels.

Mr. Barkin raised his eyebrows. "So you've always been a piece of work, huh, Stoppable?" he said.

Ron frowned. "They were bigger then," he said.

"Sure you weren't just smaller?" Mr. Barkin asked.

"They were bigger," Ron said firmly.

"Well, it looks like we're stuck for the night. Let's make the best of it," Kim said.

"Yes. Right. Follow me," said Ron. He grabbed the flashlight out of Kim's hand and led the group to the camp's old fire pit. The cheerleaders collected wood. Then Kim, Mr. Barkin, and Ron set to work. Soon they were warming their hands around a crackling campfire.

But Ron wouldn't sit by the fire. Instead, he patrolled the clearing, flashlight in hand, telling horror stories about his summer at Camp Wannaweep. Every time a cricket chirped, Ron leaped into the air like he'd been poked with a hot stick.

"I was trapped, hiding in the hollow of a

tree," Ron told the cheerleaders. "And then the woodpeckers came."

Bonnie leaned over to Kim. "Your freaky friend is acting extrafreaky," she said.

"He's not 'freaky,' Bonnie," Kim said.

Just then, an owl hooted. Ron gasped and waved the flashlight beam in front of him like a sword.

"Well, okay, he kinda is," Kim admitted. "But it's not his fault."

"It's the curse of Camp Wannaweep," Ron said dramatically.

Tara was spooked. "What if he's right?"

she asked the other cheerleaders. "What if this place is cursed?"

"Tara, please," Kim said.

"Stoppable!" Mr. Barkin growled, as Ron accidentally shone the flashlight beam into his eyes. "You're working on my nerves."

Ron pressed his finger to his lips. "Mr. B, shhhh. We've got a rustle in the brush." He crept closer to a cluster of bushes. He was just about to part them, when Kim grabbed his arm.

"Ron, I think we've established that the squirrels mean us no harm," she whispered.

"What's that supposed to mean?" Ron snapped.

"Let's just enjoy the campfire and relax," Kim said. Gently, she guided Ron back to the fire.

As soon as they were gone, the bushes rustled again. A pair of eyes peered out. But what parted the leaves was no squirrel. It was a different kind of creature—one with two huge, slimy claws!

CHAPTER 3

Campfire Tales

An hour later, Kim was starting to think that there truly was danger at Camp Wannaweep. If Ron told one more dull story, everyone would die—of boredom!

The cheerleaders rolled their eyes as Ron launched into yet another Camp Wannaweep tale. By the time he was done, Tara was the only one still listening.

"So, you shared a cabin with a tick-infested chimp?" she asked in disbelief.

Ron nodded. "Yeah, that's right. This place holds a lot of memories for me. Some bad, some . . . no, no," he corrected himself— "*all* bad."

Kim stood up, brushing leaves from her skirt. "I . . . uh . . . I'm going to get some more firewood," she announced. She started off into the woods.

"Ooooh, K.P.," Ron called after her. "Camp Wannaweep rule number one: use the buddy system."

"Oh, I think I can handle it," Kim called back.

But Mr. Barkin jumped to his feet. "He's right, Possible. I'll go, too," he said.

"Mr. B's with the program," Ron said cheerfully.

But Mr. Barkin whispered the truth to Kim

after they walked away. "I cannot take another camp story."

"Why do you think I'm going?" Kim whispered back.

"You know, Ron," Tara said when they were gone. "I happen to think it's kind of nice here."

"Oh, really?" Ron asked. He glanced at Rufus, who was sitting on a stump next to him. Rufus crossed his front legs and scowled at Tara.

"Sure," Tara said. "I mean, the woods are, you know, woodsy. And just look at the lake. It seems so peaceful."

"Ah, yes. Lake Wannaweep," Ron said. Everyone turned to look at the lake. The water was black as ink. The reflection of a full moon

shimmered on its surface. "How I hated that lake," Ron said.

The cheerleaders groaned. "Not another story!" they cried.

But Ron ignored their pleas. He poked a stick into the glowing embers of the fire. As sparks rose into the air, Ron began his tale. "It was the very first day of camp. . . ."

From the moment he first laid eyes on Lake Wannaweep, Ron knew it was evil. The water was as thick and green as pea soup. Murky brown bubbles floated on the surface.

The whole lake smelled like a spoiled tuna-fish sandwich.

"I am not going into that water," Ron promised himself.

Unfortunately, as soon as the words left Ron's mouth, the camp counselor shouted, "All right, everybody jump in the lake!"

All the other kids leaped off the dock and did cannonballs into the water. Ron had to duck and dodge like a soldier caught in enemy fire to avoid being splashed. He tried to run away, but the thick, hairy legs of the

camp counselor blocked his path.

"What's wrong now, Stoppable?" the counselor barked.

"The lake. Have you looked at it? Have you smelled it?" Ron asked. He pinched his nose in disgust. P.U.!

"Look at Ronnie!" a voice suddenly called from the water. Ron looked over and saw a boy named Gil treading water near the dock. "The squeeb's scared of the water!" Gil jeered. He sucked in a mouthful of water and spit it at Ron.

Ron ducked behind the counselor to avoid the blast. "I am not scared," he said. "It stinks. And I'm pretty sure I've seen the fish glowing at night."

The camp counselor checked the activity roster on his clipboard. "Gil, weren't you in the morning swim group? You're supposed to be in Arts and Crafts right now," he said.

"There's no way I'm getting out to make some stupid wallet," Gil replied as he backstroked past the dock.

"You stay in there too long and you're gonna wrinkle up like a prune," the counselor warned.

"Yeah, right," said Gil. He dove under-water like a fish.

Ron grabbed the counselor's clipboard and examined the roster. "You know, I could take Gil's spot in Arts and Crafts," he suggested. "And he could have my afternoon swim. I mean, you know, for the whole sum-mer."

"Oh, fine! Whatever. Just change the activity roster!" the counselor snapped, grabbing his clipboard back. He marched away, waving his hands in the air. "We're heading for jungle law, that's all I know!"

Gil swam over to the dock and squinted up at Ron. "I still say you're a squeeb," he sneered.

"We'll see who's the squeeb at the end of the summer when you're all wrinkled up like a prune and I've got a suitcase full of hand-made wallets, pot holders, and lanyards," Ron snapped back. Turning on his heel, he headed off to Arts and Crafts.

"That was the last time I ever saw Gil," Ron said, finishing his story. He looked around the fire. The cheerleaders' eyes were glazed over with boredom. Only Bonnie was still looking at him. She wrinkled her nose as if she smelled something bad.

"So," she said to Ron, "you've been a loser for, like, ever."

CHAPTER 4

Cabin Thirteen

Out in the woods, Kim and Mr. Barkin were looking for firewood. As they walked along, Kim heard a squishing noise behind them. It sounded like wet footsteps.

"Mr. Barkin, did you hear that?" she asked.

Mr. Barkin stopped and listened. A few crickets chirped. A breeze rustled the leaves overhead. "Stoppable is gettin' to ya," he told Kim. "That's just nature's music."

35

Just then, Mr. Barkin spotted a branch on the ground. As he bent over to pick it up, two huge, slimy claws shot out of a bush and grabbed his ankles. Suddenly, Mr. Barkin's legs were yanked out from under him!

"Ooof!" Mr. Barkin grunted as he hit the ground. The thing began to drag him into the bushes. Mr. Barkin tried to scream, but a slippery claw covered his mouth.

Up ahead, Kim heard a muffled groan. She spun around. "Mr. Barkin?" she asked. But Mr. Barkin was gone.

"Mr. Barkin!" Kim called out again. "Mr. Barkin!" She looked up and down the trail, but the teacher was nowhere in sight. The forest was eerily quiet. Not even a cricket chirped.

Kim dashed back to the campfire. "Have you seen Barkin?" she asked Ron and the cheerleaders.

"Kim. Duh. Barkin's with you," Bonnie said.

"Not anymore," Kim said. She glanced around at the dark woods. She was starting to have a bad feeling.

"So where is he?" Tara asked.

"I don't know," Kim said worriedly. "There were these weird sounds. He was there. More weird sounds. Then he disappeared."

"What?" Tara cried. Her voice sounded panicky.

Kim glanced around the campfire. "Uh, where are Liz and Marcella?" she asked.

"They went to the little girls' cabin," Tara said. She pointed up the hill toward the rest rooms.

Suddenly, two piercing screams split the air. Liz and Marcella! Kim sprinted up the hill. "K.P.!" Ron cried. "Buddy system!" He chased after her with Rufus on his heels.

When Kim reached the rest room, it was empty. The air inside smelled damp and mucky, like the bottom of a lake. Kim searched the room, but there was no trace of the girls.

As she came out of the rest room, Ron raced up. "Kim." He panted. "Do I have to remind you of the importance of the buddy system?"

"It didn't help Liz and Marcella," Kim said grimly.

Suddenly, Rufus chittered loudly. Kim and Ron looked down. There in the dirt was a slimy, wet footprint. But instead of five toes, there were only three. Flaps of skin stretched between them like the web on a duck's foot.

"That's not a human footprint, Kim," Ron said nervously.

"Okay, I'm getting a little freaked out here," Kim replied.

Ron frowned. "There's only one place to go," he declared. "Cabin Thirteen."

Moments later, Kim, Ron, and the remaining cheerleaders were huddled in Ron's old cabin. "In this very cabin, I was able to survive every evil Camp Wannaweep could throw at me," Ron said. "This will be our base of operations," he told the cheerleaders.

Tara raised her hand. "Uh, Ron?"

"Yes, Tara?"

"I'm hungry," Tara said.

"Well, if we pry up the floorboard like so . . ." Ron stepped on a loose board. It

tilted like a seesaw. "We'll find my secret stash of snacks!" Ron exclaimed proudly. Hidden beneath the floor was a trove of packaged chips, crackers, and cookies.

Ron pulled out a bag of chips.

"Cool!" Tara said.

"Tara, those are ancient!" Kim cried.

"Gross!" Bonnie chimed in.

Ron ripped open the bag. "Pop-Pop Porters Food-style Pork Wafers have enough preservatives to last for decades," he said. He handed a pork wafer to Tara.

She took a tiny bite. "It's not so bad," she reported. "It's definitely . . . food *style*."

Bonnie huffed impatiently. "Great! Our squad is short two people, and there's nobody to drive us to the competition," she snapped.

The other cheerleaders stared at her. *That's* what she was worried about? Crystal grabbed Bonnie by the shoulders and shook her. "Dude, forget the competition. How are we going to survive the night? There's something out there!" she cried.

"Okay, okay, you're right," Bonnie said. She thought for a moment. "Do you think that 'something' can drive?" she asked.

"Everybody stay calm. I'm going to handle this," Kim said. "Here's the plan—"

Ron reached over and tapped Kim on the shoulder. "Uh, excuse me," he interrupted.

"What?" Kim asked.

"On the school bus, Barkin's in charge. When we're saving the world, you're in charge," Ron said. "But here, at Camp Wannaweep, *I'm* in charge."

"Ron, this is serious," Kim said.

Ron pointed at his grim expression. "Hello? Note serious face," he said.

Before Kim could say more, they heard a cry from outside. "Possible!"

Ron gasped. "Mr. Barkin!"

"He's out there. Let's go!" Kim cried. They dashed out the door, leaving the cheerleaders behind in the cabin.

Kim and Ron ran through the woods. Suddenly, they saw something coming at them through the trees. It was Mr. Barkin! But—Kim gasped. He didn't seem to have

any arms! As he ran closer, she saw that his arms were stuck to his sides in a cocoon of slimy muck.

"Possible!" he cried.

"It's okay, Mr. Barkin. We're here," Kim said. She ran over to him.

"It's—it's . . . dripping and oozing muck," Mr. Barkin said between gasps of breath.

"Mr. B, what exactly is 'it'?" Ron asked.

Mr. Barkin gagged. "Freakish," he said. "It makes me ill to visualize it."

"Oh, come on," Kim said bravely. "I'm sure I've faced worse." She eyed the revolting slime that covered Mr. Barkin's body. "Did you say *oozing muck*?" she asked nervously.

Suddenly, they heard a chorus of screams. Ron, Kim, and Mr. Barkin spun around. "It's back there!" Ron cried. The monster had found Cabin Thirteen!

CHAPTER 5

Green in the Gills

Kim, Ron, and Mr. Barkin raced to the cabin. But just as they reached it, they heard a rumbling sound. Suddenly, the front wall exploded. Green muck spewed from the cabin like lava from a volcano. Kim, Ron, and Mr. Barkin ducked behind a tree to shield themselves from the blast.

At last, it stopped. Kim peered out from behind the tree. Three walls of the cabin were still standing, but they were covered in slime. All the cheerleaders, including Liz and Marcella, were pinned to the walls like flies caught in a spider's web. And crouched in the center of the room was one ugly monster. It had glowing red eyes and a fishlike head. Its arms and legs were covered with green scales. Muck dripped from its body, leaving slimy puddles on the floor.

"That's the guy," Mr. Barkin said.

Ron grimaced. "He is freakish," he agreed.

The monster turned on Ron. "I heard that, squeeb," he snarled. "Remember me?"

Ron squinted at him. "Not really," he said. "And I gotta tell you, I think I'd remember."

The monster took a step closer. Ron could smell his rotten, fishy breath. "Oh, come on, Ronnie! Think," the monster growled. "We switched places. You took my Arts and Crafts, I took your swim time. . . ."

Ron's eyes opened wide. "Gil?" he cried.

"Gil?" Mr. Barkin said, confused.

"Gil who?" Kim asked.

The monster shook his clenched fists in the air. "Oh, I am no longer Gil! Now I am Gill!" he shouted.

Ron and Kim glanced at each other. Both names sounded the same. "Ah, what's the difference?" Ron asked.

"I added an *L*," Gill growled. "You know, as in 'gill.' As in, these things that grew on my neck when I mutated." He pointed at his throat with a sharp claw. Everyone gasped. He did have gills like a fish!

Suddenly, Gill raised his arm and fired a missile of muck. It hit Kim in the chest, gluing her to a tree. "K.P.!" Ron cried. He ran to help her. But Gill stepped between them.

"Step away from Miss Possible, Ronnie," he told Ron.

Ron was startled. "How do you know her?" he asked.

"Oh, I know all about your life, squeeb. It's been going great, hasn't it?" Gill sneered.

"I—I've got some complaints," Ron said. "But who doesn't?"

"Is one of your complaints that you're a stinkin' mutant?" Gill roared.

Mr. Barkin hurried over. "All right, son," he said to Gill. "Let's take a time-out here before things get out of hand."

Gill spun around and fired another blast of muck. It knocked Mr. Barkin backward and pinned him to a pine tree.

"Do you mind?" Gill said. "Can't you see I'm catching up with my old camp buddy?"

He turned back to Ron. "So, Ron, did you ever hear why they shut down the camp?"

"Uh, no," said Ron.

Gill laughed, but he didn't sound happy. "Oh, you're gonna love this," he said. "It turns out the lake had been polluted by runoff from the science camp." He pointed a webbed finger at a camp on the far side of the lake.

"I thought that was the band camp," Ron said.

"No, that's the band camp," Gill said. He pointed to another camp. A flag marked with a musical note waved above it.

Ron frowned, puzzled. "Really? I thought that was clown camp," he said.

"No, that's clown camp," Gill snarled. He pointed to a colorful, polka-dotted circus tent on the lakeshore.

Ron chuckled. "Oh, yeah," he said. "I loved those clowns."

"Argh!" Gill growled in frustration. "The point is, the lake was toxic."

"See, I thought that lake was funky," Ron said. "I'm glad I never went in. You, on the other hand, you practically . . . lived . . . in that . . . water." Ron gulped.

"While *you* made wallets," Gill said, seething with anger.

"And lanyards," Ron added sheepishly. He pulled a woven key chain from his pocket and showed it to Gill. "I ruled at lanyards."

"Look," Kim said,

trying to reason with Gill. "We know plenty of scientists. Maybe someone can cure you."

"Science?" Gill screamed. "Science made me like this!"

Ron shook his head. "Are you sure it wasn't the clowns?"

Gill smiled evilly. "Aren't you wondering how I jammed all of your communications?" he asked.

"Equipment stolen from telecommunications camp?" Kim asked.

Gill's smile vanished. "Lucky guess," he snapped.

"So you were behind the blowout on the bus and everything," Kim said. "Why?"

Gill glared at Ron. "All part of my plan to have revenge against Ron Stoppable," he said.

"Part of me is terrified," Ron said. "And yet part of me is flattered."

"Did I mention that contact with this muck will turn you into a mutant?" Gill asked.

The cheerleaders gasped. Kim looked down at the slimy ooze that pinned her

body. "Well, you left that part out," she said angrily.

"This is sick and wrong!" Mr. Barkin cried. He struggled against the muck, but it held him tight.

"Gah!" Bonnie shrieked. "There is no way they're gonna let a squad of mutant cheerleaders in the competition!"

"There *is* no competition!" Gill roared. "Don't you get it? It was all a trap!" He turned to Ron. His fishlike lips curled in a sinister sneer. "And guess what, Ronnie? You're next!"

CHAPTER 6

Out of Muck

Gill stared Ron down with his glowing red eyes. He took one squishing step closer. Then another. Then another.

Ron started to back away. He chuckled nervously. "Hey, Gill. Maybe this is a good time to sing the Camp Wannaweep Friendship Song," he suggested.

Suddenly, Gill opened his mouth. But what came out was not a friendship song. It was a cannonball of green muck!

"Gaaaah!" Ron screamed. He dodged the muck and dove between Gill's legs. Rufus followed right behind him.

Gill whipped around and fired another blast at Ron. "Give it up, Ronnie," he snarled.

"Not when I've got my old Cabin Thirteen escape tunnel handy!" Ron cried. He pulled open a secret trapdoor in the cabin floor. *Splat!* The muck hit the door. Ron and Rufus dove into the secret passage and disappeared.

"He's ditching us!" Bonnie screamed furiously.

"That ditcher!" Tara said, disgusted.

"Ron does not ditch!" Kim told them. "He's . . ." Suddenly, she heard Mr. Barkin groan. Kim looked over. The teacher was

craning his neck as if his collar were too tight. "Mr. Barkin, what's up with you?" Kim asked.

"My neck feels all weird and itchy," he said. Suddenly, the skin on his neck turned into fish scales! "Cheese and crackers!" Mr. Barkin cried. "I'm mutating!"

Meanwhile, Ron and Rufus had followed a secret underground tunnel to the Arts and Crafts cabin. They popped up beneath a bearskin rug on the cabin floor. Quickly, Ron climbed into the room. He dragged the rug right along with him.

On the craft shelves, Ron found rolls of thin leather string used for making lanyards. He snatched up several rolls and stuffed them into a sack.

Just then, they heard a squelching foot-step. "Uh-oh," Rufus murmured. Suddenly, Gill burst through the floorboards! Opening his mouth, he pelted the cabin with a machine gun–like blast of green muck. The muck punctured the cabin door and blew out the windows. It shattered a row of clay pots on the wall. Ron and Rufus hid beneath the bearskin rug.

At last, Gill stopped to catch his breath. He looked around the cabin and spotted Ron huddled beneath the rug by the window. Gill grabbed the rug, shouting, "Gotcha, squeeb!"

But all he found underneath was an old wooden totem pole. Gill looked out the window and growled. Ron and Rufus had escaped!

Not far away in Camp Wannaweep's boat-house, Ron and Rufus were hard at work. While Rufus fixed an old boat motor, Ron made a lanyard. By the light of a dim lantern,

Ron carefully wove together the leather strings, remembering the steps he'd learned in Arts and Crafts class.

"Mr. Rabbit comes out of his hole," Ron reminded himself as he pulled a string through a loop. "He hops around a tree and . . ."

Finally, they were done. Together, Ron and Rufus pushed the motorboat out onto the lake. But when Ron pulled the engine cord, the motor only spluttered. He tried again, but it wouldn't start. "This does not bode well," Ron said.

Rufus hopped up next to the motor and kicked it with his tiny foot. The motor roared to life.

"Go, Rufus!" Ron cheered.

Meanwhile, Gill had returned to Cabin Thirteen. He was furious that Ron had escaped. He paced back and forth between the cheerleaders, trying to think where Ron might be hiding. "So he ditched you," he said.

"He did not ditch us, okay?" Kim

snapped. "He obviously—" Suddenly, they heard the roar of a boat engine out on the lake. It sounded like it was going *away* from the camp. "Found a motorboat," Kim continued. "So he could . . . uh . . . ."

"Totally ditch us," Bonnie finished for her. She glared at Kim.

Gill smiled. "He's out on the lake? *My* lake? How dumb can he be?" he cried. Squishing like a jellyfish, Gill hurried out of the cabin.

Kim slumped against her tree. Had Ron really ditched them? She glanced over at Mr. Barkin, who was gasping for air. He seemed to be having trouble breathing. "I'm getting gills!" he wheezed.

Kim gulped. She crossed her fingers that Ron hadn't ditched them. Now he *really* was their only hope.

Out on the lake, Gill slipped silently through the dark water. He could see Ron's motorboat up ahead. The boat was fast, but Gill was faster. He leaped through the water like a dolphin, gaining on Ron with every bound. Finally, he was right under the boat.

Suddenly, to Gill's surprise, the boat stopped! Gill swam to the surface. He heard Ron's panicked voice cry, "Rufus, didn't you check to see if we had enough gas!"

"Uh-oh," Rufus said.

With a roar, Gill lunged out of the water and grabbed the side of the boat. "Hey, Ron," he growled. "It's free swim." He started to rock the boat violently.

But before he could tip it, Ron said, "You're on!" He dove into the lake. A second later, Ron came up gasping for air. He wiped the toxic water from his eyes. "Okay, that water is way too funky," he said.

"Ya think?" Gill said. He circled Ron like a shark closing in on its prey. "You can't win, Ronnie," he sneered. "This is my element." Gill tackled Ron, pushing him underwater. He tried to hold him down, but Ron kicked Gill away. Gill didn't notice the loop of a lanyard lasso slip around his ankle.

Ron bobbed to the surface. "And Arts and Crafts is *my* element!" he cried. He yanked the lanyard out of the water, pulling the lasso tight.

"Hey!" Gill cried.

Ron smiled. "*Now*, Rufus!" he called. Rufus started the motorboat engine. As the

motorboat jerked forward, Rufus dove into the water.

Gill looked around, confused. "What's going on?" he cried. "You were out of gas!"

"Psych!" Rufus squeaked. Just then the lanyard line pulled tight. It was tied to the back of the motorboat! Gill was yanked through the water like a fish caught on a hook. He'd been tricked!

The pilotless boat whipped around the lake, dragging Gill behind it. It bounced off a buoy floating in the water. *Wham!* Gill smashed into the buoy. But the boat didn't stop. The buoy had turned it around, and now it was headed straight for the boathouse!

CRASH! The boat hit the dock and launched into the air, pulling Gill with it.

SMASH! The boat plowed into the middle of the boathouse and stopped. Gill flopped onto the splintered dock. He lay there gasping for air.

Ron looked down at Gill and smiled. "Free swim's over," he said.

CHAPTER 7

Ron Rocks!

As soon as he'd captured Gill, Ron jogged to the nearby telecommunications camp and phoned the police. When the police arrived, they were astonished by what they saw: a hideous muck monster trapped in a net made entirely of lanyards! Gill clawed at the net, but the lanyards were as strong as steel.

"Let me tell ya," Ron said, as Gill thrashed around helplessly. "Ron Stoppable makes a mean lanyard."

When the policemen saw the cheerleaders and Mr. Barkin trapped in the muck, they called in the biohazard team. The biohazard technicians sprayed everyone with a glowing chemical that dissolved the muck. Luckily for Mr. Barkin, it also reversed the mutation process.

"Hurry, man!" Mr. Barkin cried as a technician sprayed him down. "My feet are webbing as we speak!"

The sun was rising by the time everyone had been cleaned off. Kim and Ron watched as the biohazard scientists dropped Gill into a giant fishbowl. "Ron, you are still a squeeb!" Gill cried through the glass. "And you always will be!"

Kim introduced Ron to a scientist named Dr. Lurkin. To Ron's surprise, Dr. Lurkin actually looked happy to see Gill. "Dr. Lurkin specializes in genetic mutations," Kim explained.

"So, do you think you can reverse Gill's mutation?" Ron asked him.

"Well, I specialize in genetically altered rutabagas, so this should be quite a challenge," Dr. Lurkin replied.

Gill swam over to the side of the fishbowl and shook his fist at Ron. "I will have my revenge!" he shrieked.

Dr. Lurkin patted Ron on the back. "Oh, don't worry," he said. "I'll fix him up."

The biohazard team loaded Gill's fishbowl onto the back of a truck. "Get normal soon!" Ron called as they drove him away.

Mr. Barkin hurried over and tapped Dr. Lurkin's shoulder. "Hey, hey, check my neck," he said. He pulled his collar away so Dr. Lurkin could see. "Everything cool?" Mr. Barkin asked.

Dr. Lurkin smiled and nodded yes.

* * *

At Camp Wannaweep's front gates, Kim found Officer Hobble writing his police report. "Nice work, Miss Possible," he said when he saw her. He was used to arresting the villains that Kim captured on her missions.

Kim smiled. "Actually, Officer Hobble, it was all Ron," she replied.

"Ha-ha," the officer chuckled. "Good one, young lady."

"I'm serious," Kim said.  Just then, Ron walked out of the camp. Officer Hobble's mouth fell open in surprise. Ron was surrounded by cheerleaders! And they were all congratulating him!

"Excellent, Ron!" "All right!" "You rule!" the cheerleaders cried.

"Nice work, Stoppable," Mr. Barkin said, slapping Ron on the back.

Rufus stood on Ron's shoulder, bowing. "Thank you. Thank you," he squeaked.

"No, no, no, thank you, thank you," Ron said, bowing proudly. Tara dashed over and gave Ron a kiss on the cheek. Ron blushed.

Finally, Bonnie walked over to Ron. She blew a strand of hair out of her eyes and squinted at him. "You know, it's not like you're not still, you know, *you*," she said. "But it would really stink if that jerk had

turned us into mutants." She folded her arms. "And you were kind of brave and all," she admitted.

Ron grinned. "Who rocks?" he said.

Bonnie sighed. "You do," she said grudgingly.

"Hey, listen up!" Mr. Barkin shouted. "The police are going to give us a lift home. Let's lock and load."

"I'll be there in a minute, Mr. B," Ron called.

As the cheerleaders climbed into the police cars, Ron walked back into Camp Wannaweep for one last look at Cabin Thirteen.

Morning sunlight streamed through the huge hole Gill had blasted in the cabin's roof. Only a few boards remained of the cabin's

walls. Ron climbed the steps. It was amazing, he thought, but he would actually sort of miss this place.

"Pretty amazing," a voice said, echoing his thoughts. Ron turned around. Kim was standing behind him, smiling.

"What do you mean?" Ron asked.

"Everything!" Kim exclaimed. "You were awesome!"

Ron smiled. "Yeah. This is the one place where I know the score," he said, "where Ron Stoppable knows what it takes to be the last camper standing." Suddenly—*crack!*—the step Ron was standing on broke. Ron fell down and landed in a heap.

Kim knelt down and helped him up. "Ron, the stuff you did . . . you were resourceful. You were brave. That doesn't have anything to do with this place. It's you," she said.

"You think so?" Ron asked. A proud grin stretched across his face.

"Mm-hmm." Kim nodded.

"So, on our next mission *I* call the shots?" Ron asked hopefully.

"Ah, we'll see," Kim said. She turned and started walking back to the police cars.

Ron chased after her. "Oh, c'mon!" he cried. "I know what that means!"

"It means 'we'll see,'" Kim said.

Ron rolled his eyes and said, "Yeah, that's a code for 'not a chance.'"

"Actually, it's code for 'ferociously unlikely,'" Kim replied with a smile.

"Oh, man!" Ron whined. Kim laughed, and together they walked out to the road, leaving Camp Wannaweep behind—for good.

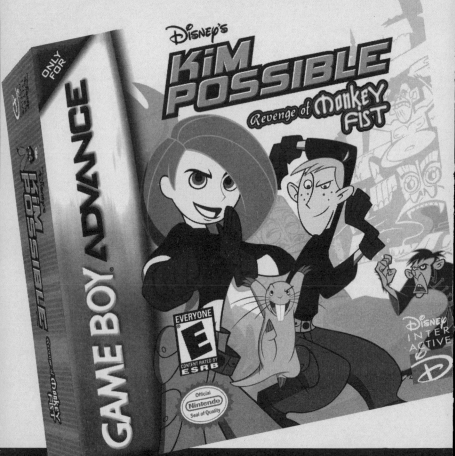